THE
BLACK KNIGHT

The
Black Knight

by Mick Gowar
and Graham Howells

Evans

First published 2008
Evans Brothers Limited
2A Portman Mansions
Chiltern St
London WIU 6NR

Reprinted 2011

British Library Cataloguing in Publication Data
 Gowar, Mick, 1951-
   The black knight. - (Skylarks)
   1. Children's stories
   I. Title
   823.9'14[J]

ISBN: 978 0 237 53580 3 (HB)
ISBN: 978 0 237 53592 6 (PB)

Printed by Guangzhou Fung Choi Fast Printing Co., Ltd in China,
September 2011, Job number 1692

Series Editor: Louise John
Design: Robert Walster
Production: Jenny Mulvanny

Contents

Chapter One   7

Chapter Two   12

Chapter Three   19

Chapter Four   27

Chapter Five   36

Chapter Six   40

Chapter One

At the edge of the village of
Wandlebury is an inn called *The Green
Man*. Weary travellers can rest at the
inn and have a meal, a drink and a bed
for the night.

On top of the hill behind the inn is an
ancient fort. It doesn't look much like a

fort. The walls fell down long ago. All that's left is a circle of bare earth surrounded by ditches. The people of the village never go up the hill to the old fort. This is why.

There was once a boy called Tom, who lived at the inn. Tom's uncle was the innkeeper. Tom worked all day as a potboy. He collected the empty mugs and plates from the tables and washed them up. Tom had never been to school, but he dreamed of leaving the village. Travellers from far away often stayed at the inn and Tom loved listening to their stories. He wanted to travel and see all the wonderful places he'd heard about for himself.

One dark night a stranger came into the inn. Some of the men in the inn

were drinking, some were eating, and
some were singing a silly song. But they
all stopped what they were doing and
stared at the stranger. His face was
unshaven and dirty. He was dressed in a
ragged patched cloak.

"What do you want?" asked the innkeeper, suspiciously. He didn't like strangers, particularly if they looked like beggars.

"A pint of ale, a meal and a bed for the night," replied the stranger.

"How are you going to pay for them?" the innkeeper asked.

"I'll tell you a story," said the stranger, "about a wonderful treasure hidden near here. If you like my story, my bed and meal will be payment. What do you say?"

"Treasure?" whispered one old man.

"Let's hear this story!" shouted a red-faced man who was sitting by the fire.

The innkeeper shrugged. "Alright," he said. "We'll hear your story."

So the stranger sat down and began his story.

Chapter Two

"Long ago, this land was ruled by King Arthur. Arthur had a group of knights who helped him. These were the famous Knights of the Round Table. They met together around a round table at Camelot, King Arthur's castle. But Arthur's greatest helper was the wizard

Merlin. Merlin used his magic to see
into the past and future. Merlin knew
what everybody in the kingdom was
doing, thinking or saying.

"Merlin brought King Arthur many magical treasures. The first treasure Merlin gave King Arthur was the magical sword, Excalibur. The second was a cloak that made the wearer invisible. The third was a golden chariot that could travel anywhere. There were thirteen great treasures in all, and their magic helped King Arthur in many of his adventures.

"But some of the knights began a war against King Arthur. They wanted the wonderful treasures for themselves.

"Merlin knew King Arthur would lose the war. So, before the last battle, he took the great treasures and hid each of them in a secret hiding place."

The storyteller paused.

"And one of those wonderful treasures

– a golden chariot pulled by a magical horse, that can take a traveller anywhere in the blink of an eye – is buried right here in the old fort, on top of the hill."

Tom the potboy gasped. The wonderful chariot that could take a traveller anywhere they wanted to go! Here in Wandlebury!

Some of the men in the inn leapt to their feet.

"Let's go and get it now!" shouted one. He pointed to the storyteller. "You can come and show us where it's buried.

We'll all be rich!"

The storyteller shook his head. "Wait," he said. "There are two things I haven't told you. First, the treasure is guarded. Not by any mortal, but by the Black Knight. He was once the bravest and greatest knight in Arthur's kingdom, and he's ten times stronger than any living knight. You can only win the treasure by challenging the Black Knight to single combat and beating him. Hanging from a tree at the top of the hill is an ancient horn. You must blow the horn and cry, 'Come out and face me knight to knight!'"

The stranger leaned forward.

"How many of you have ever defeated a fully-armed knight in battle?"

No one answered.

"Second," the storyteller continued, "he can only be defeated by someone who knows no fear. And how many of you have never been frightened, ever in your life? Is there any man here who isn't frightened of his wife?"

The men laughed.

"Is there anyone here who could challenge the Black Knight?" asked the stranger.

The men shook their heads sadly. No one noticed the door open and a small figure slip out of the inn.

Chapter Three

Tom shivered. It was very cold outside.
A full moon was shining down out of a
clear, black sky. Frost sparkled on the
ground. Tom turned his back on the inn
and began to walk up the narrow path
to the old fort.

The path was dark. Twisted trees

hung down creating a canopy and shutting out the moonlight. Tom shivered. Would he be brave enough to fight the Black Knight? He was sure he would. Tom could sense powerful magic all around him.

Tom was startled by a rustling sound. Was it the Black Knight?

No. A tiny bird – a wren – was caught in a net.

"Help me!" cried the little bird. "Please, help me!"

"You can speak," said Tom, amazed.

"Of course," said the wren. "Merlin's magic is very strong here. You will be able to understand the speech of any creature.

"I know you seek the golden chariot hidden at the old fort. If you set me free,

I can help you."

"I can't see how a tiny things like you can help me," said Tom. "But I'll free you anyway."

Tom bent down and untied the net.

The wren flew up and settled on a branch above Tom's head.

"If you need my help," said the wren, "all you have to do is call me. Just whistle these notes..."

The bird sang sweetly and flew off into the night.

Tom continued climbing. Suddenly, he heard a noise. He looked down. Just ahead of him was a hare, caught in a poacher's snare.

"Help me!" cried the hare. "The man who left this trap will be back soon. Then I'll be for the pot!"

Tom hesitated.

"Please help me," begged the hare. "I know you seek the golden chariot hidden at the old fort. If you set me free, I can help you."

"I can't see how you could help me," said Tom. "But I'll free you anyway."

Tom bent down and gently freed the hare's leg.

"If you need my help," said the hare, "all you have to do is call out to me. Just like this…"

The hare made a wailing noise and darted away into the night.

Tom started to climb again. Then, to his left, he heard a growl, and a frightened clucking sound.

A fox had cornered a cockerel in the bottom of a ditch. The fox was closing in for the kill.

"Help me! Help me!" begged the terrified cockerel.

"Don't listen to him," said the fox. "I've got three hungry cubs to feed, and he'll do nicely!"

"I know you seek the golden chariot hidden at the old fort," cried the cockerel. "If you help me, I'll help you."

"I can't see how you can help me," said Tom. "But I'll help you anyway."

Tom picked up a stick and beat the ground with it. "Get away!" he yelled. The fox ran off.

"Thank you so much," said the cockerel. "And if you ever need my help just crow like me..."

And he flapped away to shelter in some bushes.

Chapter Four

At last Tom saw the remains of the old
fort. It was bathed in moonlight. A few
metres to his right, Tom noticed an old
twisted tree. Hanging from the bottom
branch was an ancient curved horn.
Tom put the horn to his lips and blew.
A deep note blared out into the still air.

Tom shouted, "Come out and face me – knight to knight!"

There was a rumbling sound that grew louder and louder. The ground on the far side of the fort suddenly burst open, and out of the hole leapt a huge black horse with a knight in the saddle. The knight's armour was black.

The knight pulled up his horse in the centre of the circle of moonlight.

"Who dares to challenge me to single combat?" he boomed.

Tom drew his dagger from his belt.

"I do!" he replied.

"You!" sneered the knight. "You – a mere boy – dare to challenge me?"

The Black Knight leapt from his horse and began to circle Tom. Tom's heart pounded in his chest, but he held out his

dagger to show he wasn't afraid. The Black Knight rushed at Tom knocking him to the ground.

Then the ghostly Black Knight raised his huge black sword above his head.

"Do you yield to me?" he boomed.

Tom hesitated. He knew he was no match for the knight. Then he remembered the creatures he'd saved. Maybe it was true? Maybe they could help him? Tom made a high-pitched warbling whistle like a bird.

The Black Knight staggered back. He dropped his sword and began flapping his hands in front of his face. The wren was beating her tiny wings in front of the slits in the Black Knight's helmet so he couldn't see.

The Black Knight tore off his helmet. The wren flew off.

"So, you'd try to trick me with magic, would you?" bellowed the Black Knight. He ran to his horse and untied his great battleaxe from the saddle.

The Black Knight turned and rushed at Tom. Before Tom could think what to do, the Black Knight knocked him off his feet with such force that Tom's dagger flew out of his hand.

Then the Black Knight knelt beside Tom and raised his huge axe.

"Do you yield to me?" he boomed.

Tom remembered the hare. He made a loud wailing cry.

"Urgh! Argh!" yelled the Black Knight. He dropped his axe and rolled away spluttering and choking and rubbing his eyes. The hare, with her strong back legs, was kicking dirt into his face.

The Black Knight stood up and spat.

"So, you'd try to trick me with magic again, would you?" he bellowed. He ran to his horse and untied his great spiked mace from the saddle.

Desperately Tom looked around for his dagger. He couldn't see it. A shiver of fear ran down his spine. Tom picked up a fallen branch. "Come and fight me – knight to knight!" he called.

With a great roar the Black Knight ran at Tom, waving the great spiked mace over his head. He swung it at Tom's head. Tom ducked. But the ground was wet underfoot, and Tom slipped and fell.

"You won't get away again," hissed the Black Knight. "Now answer! Do you yield to me?"

Chapter Five

The Black Knight raised his mace above
his head. Remembering the cockerel,
Tom made a loud crowing sound.
   It was answered by the cockerel.
   The Black Knight froze.
   The cockerel crowed again.
   The Black Knight ran to his horse.

The cockerel crowed a third time.
The Black Knight turned to Tom.
"Day is about to break. Like all
immortals, I can only be in your world
in the hours of darkness. I must go now,
but the treasure is still mine! You did
not defeat me, either by strength or by
magic. But you showed courage, boy –
great courage." He lifted his sword in a
salute. "You are indeed worthy to be
called a knight!"

He brought the sword down in an arc and struck the ground. The earth opened, and horse and rider plunged back into their dark hiding place beneath the fort.

Chapter Six

One dark night, thirty years later, a
stranger came into the same inn at the
bottom of the hill, in the shadow of the
old fort. Some of the men in the inn
were drinking, some were eating, and
some were singing a silly song. But they

all stopped what they were doing and stared at the stranger. His face was unshaven and dirty. He was dressed in a ragged patched cloak.

"What do you want?" asked the young innkeeper, suspiciously.

"A pint of ale, a meal and a bed for the night," replied the stranger.

The innkeeper looked at the stranger's ragged clothes.

"How are you going to pay for them?" he asked.

"My name is Tom," said the stranger, "and I'll tell you a story about a wonderful treasure hidden near here. It's a true story – I can promise you that. And if you like my story, my bed and meal will be payment. What do you say...?"

If you enjoyed this story, why not read another *Skylarks* book?

Ghost Mouse

by Karen Wallace and Beccy Blake

When the new owners of Honeycomb Cottage move in, the mice that live there are not happy. They like the cottage just as it is and Melanie and Hugo have plans to change everything. But the mice of Honeycomb Cottage are no ordinary mice. They set out to scare Melanie and Hugo away. They *are* ghost mice after all, and isn't that what ghosts do best?

Yasmin's Parcels

by Jill Atkins and Lauren Tobia

Yasmin lives in a tiny house with her mama and papa and six little brothers and sisters. They are poor and hungry and, as the oldest child, Yasmin knows she needs to do something to help. So, she sets off to find some food. But Yasmin can't find any food and, instead, is given some mysterious parcels. How can these parcels help her feed her family?

Muffin

by Anne Rooney and Sean Julian

One day, Caitlin finds a baby bird sitting in a broken eggshell. She takes the bird home to the lighthouse and decides to call him Muffin. Muffin is very happy being fed tasty slivers of fish and sleeping in the cosy sock Caitlin has given him, but the time comes when every baby bird must learn to look after itself and Caitlin has to set Muffin free...

Tallulah and the Tea Leaves

By Louise John and Vian Oelofsen

It's the school holidays and Tallulah is bored, bored, BORED! That is, until her Great Granny comes to stay. Tallulah doesn't like Great Granny very much. Not very much at all, really. But, when Great Granny reads the tea leaves, things start to change and Tallulah finds herself in one adventure after another. Suddenly she isn't quite so bored anymore…

Skylarks titles include:

Awkward Annie
by Julia Williams and Tim Archbold
HB 9780237533847 / PB 9780237534028

Sleeping Beauty
by Louise John and Natascia Ugliano
HB 9780237533861 / PB 9780237534042

Detective Derek
by Karen Wallace and Beccy Blake
HB 9780237533885 / PB 9780237534066

Hurricane Season
by David Orme and Doreen Lang
HB 9780237533892 / PB 9780237534073

Spiggy Red
by Penny Dolan and Cinzia Battistel
HB 9780237533854 / PB 9780237534035

London's Burning
by Pauline Francis and Alessandro Baldanzi
HB 9780237533878 / PB 9780237534059

The Black Knight
by Mick Gowar and Graham Howells
HB 9780237535803 / PB 9780237535926

Ghost Mouse
by Karen Wallace and Beccy Blake
HB 9780237535827 / PB 9780237535940

Yasmin's Parcels
by Jill Atkins and Lauren Tobia
HB 9780237535858 / PB 9780237535971

Muffin
by Anne Rooney and Sean Julian
HB 9780237535810 / PB 9780237535933

Tallulah and the Tea Leaves
by Louise John and Vian Oelofsen
HB 9780237535841 / PB 9780237535964

The Big Purple Wonderbook
by Enid Richemont and Helen Jackson
HB 9780237535834 / PB 9780237535957

Noah's Shark
by Alan Durant and Holly Surplice
HB 9780237539047 / PB 9780237538910

The Emperor's New Clothes
by Louise John and Serena Curmi
HB 9780237539085 / PB 9780237538958

Carving the Sea Path
by Kathryn White and Evelyn Duverne
HB 9780237539030 / PB 9780237538903

Merbaby
by Penny Kendal and Claudia Venturini
HB 9780237539078 / PB 9780237538941

The Lion and the Gypsy
by Jillian Powell and Heather Deen
HB 9780237539054 / PB 9780237538927

Josie's Garden
by David Orme and Martin Remphry
HB 9780237539061 / PB 9780237538934